Nutmeg Says

YUM!

Caroline Jayne Church

ORCHARD BOOKS

Nutmeg was in the garden making a daisy chain.

"Are you hungry, Nutmeg?" called Mum.

"What would you like to eat?"

"Shall we pick some apples from the tree?"

"No," replied Nutmeg.
"Apples are too crunchy."

"Then how about some pears?"
said Mum.

"Pears are a funny colour."
Nutmeg shook her head.

"Then how about peaches?"
asked Mum,
in a very patient voice.

"Peaches are too rough,"
answered Nutmeg.

"What about bananas?" asked Mum.

"No, thank you," replied Nutmeg.
"Bananas are far too squidgy!"

Mum looked
a little puzzled.

"You don't want apples . . .
they are too crunchy.

You don't want pears . . .
they are a funny
colour.

You don't want
peaches . . .
they are too rough!

And you don't want bananas . . .
they are too squidgy.

So, what DO you want to eat, Nutmeg?" asked Mum.

Nutmeg thought for

a moment . . .

"STRAWBERRIES!"

"I'll make a special Strawberry Surprise,

just for you, Nutmeg," said Mum.

Mum started chopping and peeling,
slicing and dicing, as she prepared the
very special Strawberry Surprise.

Nutmeg skipped off to finish
her daisy chain.

"Wow!"

YUM
YUM YUM
YUM YUM
YUM

YUM!

Nutmeg ate it all up!

"I'm going to call this

NUTMEG'S RAINBOW TREAT!"

She gave Mum a big hug and said,
"Thank you for my Rainbow Treat . . .
please can we make it again tomorrow?"